DEDICATED TO LOVED ONES - YOURS AND OURS -
PAST, PRESENT AND FUTURE.
Richard M. Wainwright & Ron Walotsky

FAMILY LIFE
PUBLISHING

FAMILY LIFE
PUBLISHING
RICHARD M. WAINWRIGHT BOOKS
87 Rebecca Road
Scituate, MA 02066

Box 353844
Palm Coast, FL 32135

web site - www.rmwainwrightbooks.com

Printed in Singapore by Tien Wah Press, Published in the United States of America 2000
Sculpture of child's head, "Jade," by Peter A. Cerreta

Library of Congress Cataloging-in-Publication Data
Wainwright, Richard M.
MESSENGERS / written by Richard M. Wainwright: illustrated by Ron Walotsky-1st ed.
p. cm.
Summary: Tormented by unanswered questions about his adoption and his Asian heritage, fifteen-year-old Tyler has a spiritual experience that leads him to a shelter for the homeless and changes his life.
ISBN# 1-928976-00-X (hardcover : alk. Paper)
[1. Conduct of life Fiction.   2. Homeless persons Fiction.   3. Adoption Fiction.
4. Asian Americans Fiction.] I. Walotsky, Ron, ill. II. Title.
PZ7.W1317Me 2000
[Fic] -- dc21   99-36488
CIP

Messengers

Written by Richard M. Wainwright
Illustrated by Ron Walotsky

TO: *Brian*

Never forget,
your love can make a difference.

With best wishes,

Ron Walotsky   Richard M. Wainwright

With all good wishes –
your friend,
Richard M. Wainwright
2001

FROM: *Mom and Dad with love!*

Chapter I

The street light created an eerie glow in the bedroom. Tyler Lee Smith stared at the same spot on the dimly lit ceiling for possibly the one thousandth time. He would have preferred to go to sleep immediately. His body was tired enough but his mind was wide-awake. It had been like this for several years. The litany that obsessed him wouldn't go away. Do my parents really love me? Do they love Sarah more than me? What would my life have been like today if I hadn't been adopted? Why did my real parents give me up? Would I be happier among my own people? What do my classmates really think of me? Am I their token Oriental? Do teachers grade me differently because of my race? These questions made him angry and bitter, and with some intensity he carried these emotions with him every minute of every day.

Tyler was part Filipino and part Chinese. He had no idea how much of each. Tall and thin for his age, he had a slightly tan complexion with black hair and striking green Asian eyes. If strangers had been asked to describe Tyler, they would have replied, "He is a fine looking young man."

His earliest memory was of being held in the arms of a sobbing woman. He believed that the woman was his mother but he wasn't sure. In addition to himself, Tyler remembered several other young children clinging to the woman's skirt. Tyler thought they probably were his brother and sisters. He recalled the woman shook uncontrollably as she passed him to another lady who immediately cradled him and tried at the same time to comfort his siblings as well. The crying woman abruptly turned and fled the building, leaving all her children behind. This was Tyler's only memory of a family. Later, he learned the building was an orphanage in the Philippines. He knew nothing more of his life before his adoption.

Peggy, a teacher, and Ron, a doctor, had flown to the Philippines to adopt Tyler when he was four years old. Previously, medical tests had indicated that they probably would not be able to have children. They had been told little of Tyler's background. They were so happy just to have been able to adopt him, that all they could think of was getting Tyler back to the United States. The orphanage's director told the Smiths that Tyler had arrived two years previously. The director would not say more.

Tyler recalled his first three years with the Smiths and all the attention he had received. He had been the center of their world but his two years at the orphanage made him wary of attention and affection. He knew it could be withdrawn at any time. He remembered people in the Philippines who had cared for him and then disappeared weeks or months later.

Three years after Tyler had been adopted, Mrs. Smith became pregnant, and blond, blue-eyed Sarah was born.

Now as a teenager, he realized that even if Peggy and Ron had been his natural parents, his world would have changed after the birth of Sarah. But at the time, all he knew was his adopted parents spent a lot of time with the new member of the family and a lot less with him. He had been jealous, and withdrawn and spent more and more time alone in his room. Some nights, Tyler's memories took him back to elementary school. Mrs. Hart, his 1st grade teacher, introduced him to the world of computers and by the end of the year, Ron had bought him his own computer. Tyler spent even more time alone in his room. In the 3rd grade, his partner in the computer lab was Jason Goldman. Jason was shy and deaf but equally loved computers. At the beginning, they communicated by pointing to words. Then they wrote notes, and then Jason learned to read Tyler's lips. By the 6th grade, Tyler had learned sign language. They had a common bond— both were fascinated with cyberspace. They were kindred spirits who lived in their separate worlds when not in the computer lab.

Tyler named his first and succeeding computers "Gates" after Bill Gates, the genius founder of Microsoft. Tyler thought of his computer as his best and only real friend. Before he graduated from elementary school, the computer was a lot more than games and educational programs. He had access to the internet and an infinite amount of information. Once in a while he and Jason would chat via e-mail.

Tyler began to systematically read about the lives of the world's greatest scientists and their discoveries. His heroes became Copernicus, Curie, Salk, Ford, Fahrenheit, and Oppenheimer, to name just a few. Cyberspace pioneers like Gates, Jobs and others joined his growing list of those responsible for the technological development of the world. These people lived in his computer and became his best friends—closer to him than even his teachers, classmates or parents.

Intellectually, Tyler had no problem communicating, but he would not permit himself to care deeply for any human being. Daily, the wall around his heart grew thicker. Tyler never thought of himself as being above average or bright. He simply accepted his academic interests and abilities without comparing them to others.

In reality, he had an exceptional intellect, which had banished emotions. In school, Tyler was quiet but his academic success soon got the attention of his classmates and teachers. He spoke softly, yet with confidence. He earned respect. He never bragged when he received high grades or excelled on the athletic field.

By the time he was in junior high, his name appeared quarterly on the high-honors list. He captained the soccer team. Even with this recognition, Tyler's psychological wall ensuring emotional distance remained stronger than ever. No one else could see it, but Tyler knew it was there. With each passing day, his interaction with people became more superficial, although his behavior was always correct and friendly. At night, he stared at the ceiling asking the same unanswerable questions.

Tyler remained polite and respectful toward Peggy and Ron. He did his chores without complaint. He liked the Smiths. They were nice people but he did not love them. He felt he never had nor ever would love anyone with the exception of his birth mother. Yet, once in a while, Tyler tolerated his younger sister and occasionally played with her. Sarah's antics usually made Tyler laugh. He wouldn't admit it to himself but he enjoyed her spontaneous acts of affection. Frequently, after supper, she would run into his room while he was working on the computer, wiggle onto his lap and plead, "Tyler, please read to me?"

Tyler would put on a false frown, grumble and mutter "Kids!" fooling only himself before he began reading a book to Sarah. With the knowledge possessed by young children, Sarah saw through Tyler's indifference and detachment. Young hearts always see better than eyes.

When his homework was done, he would surf the internet for scientific information. He came to believe that science would be the world's salvation. It would eventually solve all the planet's problems. As he read, he would scribble notes. The next day, Tyler would visit the college library where his mother worked and he would sign out books. Tyler had the rare gift of a photographic memory. Words and ideas were stored in his mind as permanently as in his computer's hard drive. By the 8th grade, with his parents' blessing, he was allowed to audit one of the college's math or science courses each semester. He wasn't required to write papers or do homework but he did both. He read the assigned text, filed his papers in his computer and researched related material. Tyler never took any tests, but if he had, he would have earned A's from astonished professors.

Tyler breezed through junior high excelling academically and athletically. With his class-mates and the faculty, he laughed, smiled, nodded and listened appropriately, but his heart was always elsewhere. Students and adults thought they were close to him. They were wrong. Tyler's mind had hidden his heart far, far away from every person who was part of his life. Only Jason had made a tenuous but real connection.

Tyler's parents knew their son was bright. By the time Tyler entered the 10th grade the conversation at the dinner table ranged from helping Sarah with her 3rd grade spelling words to domestic and international politics, scientific breakthroughs in all fields, the latest computer innovations, the internet and medical discoveries. Tyler's father was an orthopedic surgeon.

As Tyler had grown older, his relationships with peers and adults became strictly intellec-tual. Now in his 15th year, Tyler had shrunk his emotions to microscopic size. They became too small for him to recognize. Others saw only a reflection of their feelings for Tyler. Relaxed in his room, in front of "Gates", Tyler absorbed gigabytes of information. He never went to bed until his eyelids closed at least twice. He didn't want to face the questions and memories that came at night.

Chapter II

Tyler had never lost his temper until the day he returned home from school to find that Sarah had turned on his computer, and had tried to insert a CD the wrong way, damaging the CD drive. There were floppies and CD's scattered on the floor. Tyler imagined her walking all over them. For the first time in his life, Tyler lost it. "How could she touch my computer—this is my room—she had no right. I. . . I hate her!" he thought.

Tyler felt he had to get out of the house. Uncharacteristicly, he thundered down the stairs. His mother heard him and knew something was wrong. She wanted to cry out, "Tyler, wait!" but didn't. She knew her son would take his bike and managed to call, "Don't forget your helmet!"

"Right!" Tyler yelled angrily. Grudgingly, and in haste, he put on his helmet. Blind with rage, he jumped on his ten-speed. In seconds, he was barreling out of his driveway toward the street. Usually it was a quiet street with little traffic—today there was a truck, a big truck. The driver barely got a glimpse of a boy on a bike directly in front of him. He applied the brakes a split second before the crash. Tyler saw a brilliant flash of white light; it enveloped him, then peace.

It was dark—darker than his room at night. Tyler thought at first he was dreaming and would wake up momentarily. Then he heard voices—they were a long way away. His eyes remained closed—his body motionless. Again, he lost consciousness.

Tyler's parents sat immobile. Their eyes were riveted on Dr. Chipman. Dr. Chipman was a neurologist.

"First of all, you should know," Dr. Chipman began, "Tyler experienced a cardiac arrest during the ambulance ride to the hospital. The EMT's got his heart going again. He received a severe blow above his right ear where the temporal lobe of the brain is located. We know this area is responsible for language, day dreaming, long-term planning and provides a link to consciousness. At this point, all we know for certain is that Tyler's brain is functioning normally but he remains unconscious. At the moment, his brain waves are strong but he suffered a tremendous blow. He is alive only because he was wearing his helmet. We have no idea at this point the true extent of the damage. Only time will allow us to make an accurate assessment. Miraculously, the rest of his body suffered only severe contusions and no broken bones. It does not appear there are any critical internal injuries, but it is impossible to estimate your son's chances. We will know much more in a week. I'm very sorry. Your son has a chance. You both must get some rest. We will do everything medically possible and notify you immediately of any changes—good or bad. At the moment, we can only hope and pray for Tyler's recovery."

The tears continued to cascade down the cheeks of the Smiths. Dr. Smith held his wife tightly. Numbly they nodded in unison as Dr. Chipman slowly rose and left the room.

During the weeks that followed, Tyler underwent several cranial operations to relieve the swelling in his brain. His parents were at his side many hours each day. The doctors did everything possible. Tyler remained in a coma.

"Peggy, Ron," Dr. Chipman began at a subsequent meeting, "there is nothing more we can do for Tyler in the hospital. His body is recovering nicely. His brain has returned to its normal size and all bleeding has stopped. There may be brain damage but we cannot measure to what extent while Tyler remains in a coma. His brain waves continue to be strong and that is a good sign. Whether or not Tyler will soon wake from the coma, no one can say. If you wish, Tyler can be moved to your home. Having family and friends around may help. It may also allow you to increase the amount of his daily physical therapy."

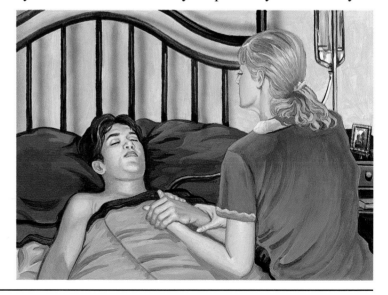

A few days later, Tyler was in his own bed. He was attached to several tubes, which fed him and carried off wastes. His parents and sister were happy to have him home.

A nurse taught Mrs. Smith how to take care of her son. Each morning, Mrs. Smith fed and bathed Tyler. When finished she would sit on the bed and tell Tyler his family loved him very much.

She told him how they had dreamed of finding a child like Tyler. Peggy described the laborious and often convoluted road they had to travel to adopt him but always added that she and her husband would have done it a hundred over to have gotten Tyler. Peggy mentioned the years of hope, frustration and the costs associated with working with adoption agencies. The money was unimportant, but their experiences of losing two children they had selected, due to government immigration rules, almost made them quit trying.

Peggy spoke of their trip to the Philippines, which was long, yet she and Ron had been too excited to sleep. Three days later, ecstatic, they left the orphanage with Tyler. They didn't sleep on the flight home either but stayed awake looking at the beautiful little boy between them.

Before leaving Tyler, Peggy would always kiss him on the forehead and tell him one more time she loved him. Her tears fell on Tyler's pillow.

Tyler heard every word.

Tyler's world was black. His memory was fine. He remembered finding his computer and room a mess and racing to his bike. He even remembered peddling down his driveway, but his eyes wouldn't open and he couldn't move. He could only hear.

Each day, Sarah would come into Tyler's room and sit next to him. She would talk about her day in school. Before she left, she would tell Tyler she loved him and carefully would give him a kiss on the cheek. Peggy and Ron spent many hours each day talking to Tyler and describing their day, news of his school and always telling him how much they loved him.

Soon Tyler's classmates and teachers began coming to assist Mrs. Smith with Tyler's physical therapy. Every day someone would come to move his arms and legs and help Dr. or Mrs. Smith change his position. Jason Goldman came twice a week. He had changed a great deal since meeting Tyler in the 3rd grade. Their relationship had given him the confidence to begin to reach out to others. Now he had many friends, was a class officer and played on the same soccer team as Tyler. Jason cared deeply for Tyler—his friend had made a big difference in his life. Before leaving Tyler's room, he always signed, "Get well—we love you."

Everyone believed some day Tyler would wake up. They talked out loud telling him of school activities while they worked. They told Tyler how much they missed him and hoped he would be back soon. Tyler listened but couldn't open his eyes. Weeks went by without a change. Tyler's parents, teachers and friends never gave up hope.

One afternoon, Mrs. Smith turned on the gas under the teakettle. She had just finished bathing and feeding Tyler. She was weary from worry, tired and discouraged. She needed a cup of tea. She hoped that somehow it would magically renew her waning strength and her sagging faith that Tyler would recover.

The doorbell rang. Mrs. Smith turned. She thought the students and teacher scheduled to work with Tyler had come a little early. Instead, when Mrs. Smith opened the door, she looked into the jade eyes of a very old Oriental man. He had a flowing white beard. His hands were clasped in front of him. He bowed, smiled and his eyes twinkled. He spoke in almost a whisper. "I have come to see Tyler—may I come in, please?"

Moments passed. Mrs. Smith realized her mouth was still open. She stared at a person about her size. He wore a gold robe, which almost touched the ground. On his head was a peculiar, colorful hat. The wrinkled face radiated gentleness and kindness. "Yes, please come in," she finally said.

Bowing again, the old man followed Mrs. Smith upstairs. She stayed at the bedroom door as the stranger shuffled to the foot of Tyler's bed. He stood silently for several minutes before he spoke. His words were soft yet firm, but Mrs. Smith could not understand him. He was speaking Mandarin.

"Tyler," the old one began, "You can hear and understand me and see me with your third eye. My name is Meng K'e. I am one of your ancestors, one of your guardians—a humble messenger. We all are messengers. We are born knowing right from wrong and that life is a journey of love. We can deny these truths, but our real nature wants to share this knowledge.

"You have learned during the past two months how much love surrounds you. Your heart knows you are loved by many people and by the Creator. Experiences and memories have convinced you to reject and fear love. Tyler, you will never lose the love of your biological parents. Love is never lost or forgotten. The love that has kept you alive has come from many sources.

"Tyler, life is a gift and how we live it is very important. You have been given much— much is expected. The quality and quantity of love we share through words and deeds are the measure of our lives. The greatest gift we can give to another is love. Every human being follows a unique path but we are here to help each other.

"Where we come from is not important. What we become is all-important. If you wish your spiritual journey to continue on earth, you must open up your heart. Ask the Creator for light. You will see."

Mrs. Smith was frozen in the doorway. She had observed the ancient man's every move. She hadn't understood a word but intuitively, she knew Tyler had been in no danger. The patriarch's mouth closed, he bowed his head and stood motionless. Then he began to move toward the door. The old one paused in front of Mrs. Smith, smiled, bowed again and began to descend the stairs. Mrs. Smith followed closely behind him. She had many questions.

The old man did not slow his measured steps as he approached the front door. He did not reach for the doorknob—he walked through the now incandescent door.

Mrs. Smith wiped her eyes. She quickly opened the closed door. Standing on the threshold, she looked right and left. No one— young or old was in sight. Had she imagined everything? Could she be so tired that she was having hallucinations? Did she need to see a doctor? . . . The teakettle began to whistle.

Chapter III

The blackness remained. Tyler's mind was racing over the experience. In his third eye, he could see Meng K'e perfectly—even his leather sandals. Every word the old man had spoken was in capital letters on his mental screen, which continued to scroll over and over again.

Evening came. Sarah entered Tyler's room. She hopped onto the bed and began telling him of her day. Finally, she stopped speaking, closed her eyes and prayed out loud asking God to make her brother well. After the "amen," she kissed Tyler and went to her room. Later, Tyler's mother and father prepared him for the night. As always, they repeated words of love for him asking that he please come back to them. Tyler's mother hadn't mentioned the afternoon visitor to her husband. She had come to believe it simply could not have happened. Both parents were exhausted. They kissed Tyler goodnight and went to bed.

Tyler's mind stayed awake. There is no night or day when all is black. Methodically, Tyler began to examine Meng K'e's words and their implications. Slowly, like taking apart a wall brick by brick, the barrier that had surrounded his heart disappeared. The unconditional love he had given and received as a baby returned to his heart. Tyler finally understood and accepted the purpose of his life. He was no longer afraid to give and receive love. He stopped thinking. His heart and mind asked, "Please! Let there be light."

The next morning Peggy and Ron dressed wearily. Peggy would get Sarah ready for school. Ron had to be in his office early. However, first they would bathe and prepare Tyler for his day. They raised his window shades and looked in disbelief at their son.

Tyler's eyes were wide open. His smile illuminated his face. "Hi Mom, Hi Dad," he whispered. His parents rushed to Tyler. They hugged him as they cried. No one said anything for a long, long time. Ron and Peggy's son was back. What they didn't know was Tyler was not the same young man who had gone away.

The day Tyler woke up was like one long birthday party. His parents and Sarah spent all day in his room. They left the room only for food when friends and a teacher came to give him physical therapy. Of course, they were thrilled to find Tyler awake. The good news spread rapidly. Lots of people came by. Tyler received hundreds of hugs, kisses, and pats from friends whose hopes and prayers had come true. Late in the afternoon, Dr. Chipman arrived.

After warmly welcoming Tyler back, Dr. Chipman thoroughly examined his patient. He told Tyler that even though he had had physical therapy consistently while in a coma, his muscles were still very weak. Tyler would continue to need physical therapy. Slowly, he could begin exercising. He discussed Tyler's return to solid food. Finally with a huge grin, Dr. Chipman predicted Tyler would make a complete recovery. "Tyler, you will be better than ever."

Tyler smiled outwardly. Inwardly, he said to himself, "Yes, Doctor, I will be much, much better."

During the following weeks, Tyler found Dr. Chipman was right. He couldn't hop out of bed, do sit-ups or push-ups. All his muscles functioned, but they were very weak. His hands and arms moved in slow motion. Getting food to his mouth took tremendous effort and concentration. His parents and friends continued to help. Tyler constantly thanked them for everything they had done for him. As he grew stronger, he took more responsibility for his physical therapy. At first, even a short effort made him very tired. He read newspapers, magazines and watched television. Soon he was up to speed on world events—getting his physical strength back would take much more time.

After exercising and reading, Tyler had free time. He turned to another interest. He had always enjoyed attempting to repair gadgets and appliances. He decided it would help bring back his finger dexterity. His parents brought several items to his bedroom. Tyler examined a talking bear of Sarah's which had been silent for over a year, a malfunctioning mini-cassette recorder of his father's and an old radio he had found on a curb waiting for the trash truck. In addition, his mother brought up a blender that had been relegated to the cellar. His special tools, electrical testing equipment, along with a box of assorted parts and supply catalogs, were placed on a bedside table.

It didn't take Tyler long to find that the audiocassette in Sarah's mute bear was broken and couldn't be fixed, but it could be replaced. Tyler had some blank tapes and recorded a personal message in his deepest voice.

"Hi, Sarah. I am your buddy Tyler Bear. Did you have a good day at school? Grrrrreat to see you. I love you. I love you!" said the stuffed bear.

Sarah was thrilled when she returned home from school to find her bear talking again with a personal message from her brother. After giving Tyler a kiss, she scampered off to show her mother.

When classmates learned what Tyler was doing as part of his physical therapy, he was inundated with old stuff. Many of these items could be fixed. Most things, he and his family or friends couldn't use. When repaired, they were given to their church's thrift shop.

Late one afternoon, Tyler's mother appeared at his bedroom door. She held a floor lamp.

"Tyler," she said, "a few minutes ago a lady came to our front door with this lamp. She is poorly dressed and appears very discouraged. She said her family needs light. A rather strange choice of words but anyway, I asked her to wait. Maybe she is the mother of one of your friends. What shall I tell her?"

A pensive look came to Tyler's face. He took the lamp from his mother. "Please tell her to wait. I will try to fix it right now."

It was a tall metal lamp with three bulbs. The shade was dusty. The base was grimy from spilled liquids. Tyler first removed the bulbs, sockets and electrical cord. He thought the lamp might be six or seven years old but the parts seemed older. For some reason they had aged faster than normal. The switches stuck. There was rust everywhere, the wiring was frayed and the plug broken. Working rapidly, Tyler replaced every suspect part: new wiring, sockets, switches, even new bulbs. He dusted the shade, cleaned and polished the metal and then plugged in the lamp. Not surprisingly, when he flipped the switches the bulbs shone brightly. He called his mother.

Mrs. Smith carried the lamp downstairs. A few minutes later, she returned to report. "Tyler, I think that lady has serious problems. While she waited she held her head in her hands and cried. When she saw I had returned with the lamp, she stood up, accepted it and muttered, 'God, help us.' She didn't say another word. Not even thanks. I watched her walk to a rather battered car. Maybe I shouldn't have let her in."

Tyler chuckled, "Mom, what happened to your Good Samaritan philosophy? We tried to help someone. No one can do more than that. I enjoyed fixing the lamp. Hopefully, it will in some way make her life a little better."

Peggy Smith smiled, nodded and left to prepare supper. She knew her son was right. She felt a little embarrassed that she had momentarily forgotten the teachings of their church.

Chapter IV

With tremendous daily effort, Tyler made rapid physical progress. Within ten weeks, he was ready to return to school. Academically, he had caught up with his classmates. His teachers had supplied a complete list of the material they had covered during Tyler's weeks in a coma. Now, after Tyler had done his homework, his time on "Gates" was divided equally reading the lives of philosophers, artists, spiritual leaders as well as scientists. He was amazed to learn the major role religion had played in world history. Zealots brought tyranny and wars. True spiritual leaders led by example and preached tolerance. It seemed the great ones asked nothing more than to serve others. Their message was basically the same. Love and care for one another.

The lives of Moses, Christ, Mohammed, Buddha, Krishna, Socrates, Confucius, Gandhi, Mother Theresa, St. Francis and other religious and philosophical giants made a deep impression on Tyler. Years later, his own library would contain copies of the Bible, the Bhagavad Gita, the Koran, the Torah, and many philosophy books.

As time passed, his parents realized the new Tyler was here to stay. He expressed his feelings. He hugged and kissed his parents and sister. Sarah couldn't have had a better brother. At school, friendships were not one-sided. He really cared about his colleagues and mentors. Just before school closed for the summer, one of his teachers, Paul McGourty, asked Tyler to speak to him after class.

"Tyler," Mr. McGourty asked, "have you heard of Habitat for Humanity?"

Tyler's blank look answered the question.

"It's a program to build homes for people who can't afford to build or buy one themselves. The future owners work alongside the volunteers, and when the house is finished, the total cost is affordable. The chosen family is able to pay the monthly mortgage payments. We have two houses scheduled for the summer. We could use your help, but it would require most of your vacation. Will you think about it?"

Tyler thought of his options for the summer: computer classes, soccer camp, family trips and free time to do research on the Philippines. He thought someday that he might go there to see if he could find any information on his birth parents, his brother and sisters. Yet, with all those things in mind, something told him to accept this offer. "Mr. McGourty, you can count on me."

Mr. McGourty was a little surprised but delighted with Tyler's quick decision. "Great. I know you'll learn fast. Here is a packet for you and your parents about Habitat and the two houses we will build. If you know any other young people who might be interested, we could use more volunteers. Thanks, Tyler. See you tomorrow."

At dinner that night, a discussion of summer plans was held. Tyler reviewed the Habitat program with his folks. His father commented with a grin that he was happy he was a doctor. He and Peggy would prepare for a summer of cuts, bumps and bruises. He added, "I'm good at setting broken bones, but I think you have spent enough time in bed for one year. Be careful on the roof."

Everyone laughed. Tyler's mother spoke next. "Tyler, I wanted to tell you something that happened last week. Do you remember when you were in bed fixing things and the day I brought you a floor lamp?"

"Yes, I remember," Tyler replied.

His mother continued, "Well, I met the lady last week in the supermarket. She spotted me. I wouldn't have recognized her. She was nicely dressed and knew my name. She told me that she had no idea why she stopped at our house to have the lamp repaired. Her life had been unhappy for a long time. Her husband was an alcoholic and, during the past several years, he had lost one job after another. He had become increasingly mean toward her and their children. The family was close to losing their home. She was at the lowest point in her life when she came to our house. When she returned home, her oldest boy took the lamp to their living room and plugged it in. She said the light worked perfectly and seemed to change the feeling in the room. She shrugged as she told me this.

"That night, for the first time in months, the woman's husband arrived home sober. He said he had been to an AA meeting and realized, if he didn't get help that he would lose his family. The children huddled behind their mother. They didn't believe him. Her husband picked up the children one by one and gently hugged and kissed them. The woman told me she sat down in shock. She laughed, saying it was a good thing because then her husband kissed her, too.

"The lady went to bed thinking it probably was all a dream but now the dream is four months old. Her husband hasn't missed a day of work, has been promoted, spends most of his free time with their children, goes to church with the family on Sundays and faithfully attends AA meetings. When she had finished telling me this story, she gave me a kiss on the cheek and walked away."

Ron Smith observed, "Amazing. Nice to hear a happy ending. Sometimes we forget people can change for the better. There's always hope."

Tyler didn't say anything. He was thinking. Quickly the conversation swung to weekend trips during the summer.

It was a very busy summer. Sarah went to day camp and that required chauffeuring. Tyler worked with Habitat during the week and also worked two nights at a local computer store. Weekends were reserved for family excursions, for pick-up soccer games and visits from relatives. Before bed, Tyler would read or computer surf.

One Sunday evening toward the end of the summer, Tyler's father commented that the family had heard regularly of Sarah's day camp activities but only bits and pieces of Tyler's life. Now, he said, would be a good time for an in-depth report. Looking at Tyler, he said, "You have our complete attention."

"Ladies and Gentlemen," Tyler began with a grin. "Unaccustomed as I am to public speaking, I will try to describe my doings and undoings. Two days a week, I have been gainfully employed by Computer World where I have shared my limited knowledge of Cyberspace with fellow employees and customers alike. The owner, inexplicably, has given me a raise and wants me to put in as many hours as possible during the school year. It's really been a fun job. I meet a lot of nice people. I am able to keep up with the latest computer technology and software. Something new arrives every day.

"Five days a week you may have noticed, I leave home in my Wranglers with a wide leather belt strapped to my waist. If you have observed closely, you have seen hanging conspicuously from my belt a standard heavy-duty claw hammer. The supervisors at Habitat wisely did not allow me to use this tool during my first weeks on the job. Initially, other volunteers and I were "gofers." First I had to master the science of fetching objects, such as 4' x 8' sheets of particle board, nails, screws, shingles, coffee and donuts. (I might add the latter items were the most difficult to deliver correctly.) Finally, I graduated to pounding nails, shingling, painting and eventually assisting drywall sheetrockers, plumbers and electricians.

"In spite of my help, the houses we began in June will be completed before school opens. Seriously, it has been one of the finest experiences of my short life. The lessons I have learned are not found in books or on web sites.

"Oh yes, besides working with many adults, there were eight other people my age, including my buddy, Jason. We all became good friends. In fact, that brings me to my piece-de-resistance. One of my co-workers is a young lady who goes to Madison High School. Her name is Maria Cugno. She is very bright, hardworking, attractive and wields a terrific paintbrush. I would like to invite her to dinner and have you all meet her. Thank you all for your attention."

The laughter and applause from Sarah and Tyler's parents were followed by immediate questions. Sarah and Tyler's mother wanted to know what Maria looked like. How old was she? What grade was she in? What were her interests? On it went.

Like a politician in front of a frenetic group of reporters, Tyler theatrically raised his hands. "Let me take one question at a time," he began. "Maria will also be a junior this year. She plans to major in languages and sociology in college. She is fluent in Japanese, Italian and Spanish and is on the varsity volleyball team and student council. Her dad's name is Charles. He's a landscape designer. Yoshi, her mother, teaches Hatha Yoga and T'ai Chi. Maria's one flaw is she seems to like me. No more questions, please."

Tyler's mother excused herself from the table and returned with the family calendar. She chided Tyler for keeping Maria a secret and jokingly suggested setting a dinner date before Maria knew Tyler better. A day was selected and after supper Tyler e-mailed Maria an invitation.

The dinner was a big success. Maria was a charming, articulate young lady with jet-black eyes and a contagious smile. She was open, obviously loved life and her family very much. Maria's grandparents, Japanese Americans, lived in California. Her dad's folks, second generation Italians, lived nearby. Maria had lived with relatives in Japan and Italy. Her parents met in a martial arts class in college. Maria's mother taught elementary school before Maria, Anthony and George arrived. Now that Maria and her brothers are in their teens, their mother is able to teach Yoga and T'ai Chi three nights a week.

After the meal, conversation continued in the kitchen until the dishes were done. Sarah immediately took Maria by the hand, leading her upstairs to introduce her to her dolls and stuffed animals. Sarah asked Maria to help her with a new level of an educational program on her computer. A half-hour later, Maria was rescued by Tyler's mother as it was bath and bed time for Sarah.

Three days before school reopened, the Habitat houses were turned over to the new owners. Maria's parents hosted a pizza party for the Habitat crews.

As they entered 11th grade, Tyler and Maria discussed possible extracurricular activities. Tyler decided to take T'ai Chi one evening a week. It just happened to be on the same night that Maria assisted her mother. After class, Maria and Tyler would get something to eat. They often talked about all they had learned the past summer. The satisfaction and enjoyment they had experienced made them want to continue volunteering. Maria signed up to tutor elementary school students one afternoon a week. Following the soccer season, Tyler volunteered to work two Saturdays a month at a shelter for the homeless in Merrelburg. Tyler would begin the following Saturday.

Sometimes at night, Tyler thought of all that had happened since his accident. The words of Meng K'e were not forgotten yet; he wondered if his imagination had created the event from a book or article he had read. Real or imagined, the experience had changed him. Now, he fell asleep as soon as he closed his eyes.

Tyler's breath condensed as he boarded the metropolitan blue bus for Merrelburg. Merrelburg was a small city compared to New York or Los Angeles, but it had over nine hundred thousand people. On the bus, he thought of the paper he had written on the homeless. It had troubled him to learn there were a huge number of human beings in the world without homes. In the United States alone there were more than one million homeless people.

Mencius House was in an old section of the city. Tyler's father had checked out its location and had spoken with the director. The bus stopped almost in front of the shelter. Tyler got off and looked up at an old three story brick building. A number of men, women and children were waiting outside the entrance. Many had their coat collars turned up. Some wore just sweaters. Tyler knew they must be cold. Several were stamping their feet. Tyler thought about the fact he was wearing a new heavy parka and lined leather gloves.

He looked up and down the street and could see other people in small groups walking toward the shelter. He felt a little self-conscious as he worked his way slowly through the small crowd of men and women toward the front door. A number were chatting amicably with a big man who radiated inner strength.

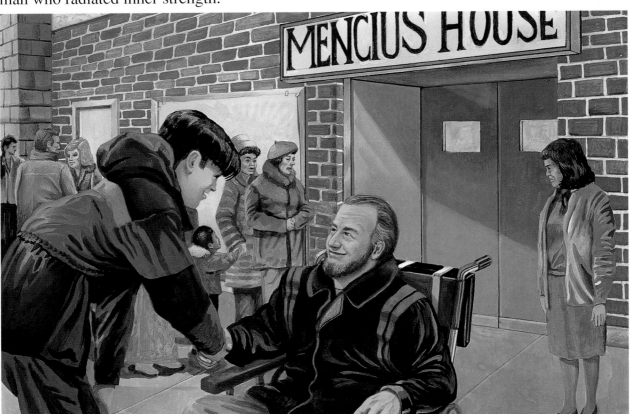

The man had a tough, craggy yet friendly face partly covered by a neatly trimmed reddish beard. He had a deep voice but his words were spoken softly. A heavy gray jacket covered his broad shoulders. He was the only person wearing fairly new clothes. He was the only person in a wheel-chair. He was the only man without feet. The man spotted Tyler.

The wheelchair-bound man raised an arm to shake hands, smiled, and spoke. "Hello, I presume you're Tyler Smith."

"Yes, sir," Tyler replied as he shook hands.

"Tyler, just call me Collector. Before you go inside, Tyler, I want you to meet some friends of mine. This is Betsy, her daughter, Felicia, and sons Nathan and Tom. These gentlemen are Gillette, Larry, Ricardo and Rabbit. You'll get to know most everyone who lives here or comes for breakfast and supper. Rabbit is working today, too. He'll introduce you to Simon Bolivar Peterson, the director. I'll see you later."

Tyler smiled, nodded and followed Rabbit through the entrance into a large room. He smelled bacon and eggs cooking. The director was busy doing paperwork at one of the tables but he stopped and warmly welcomed Tyler. He concluded with a smile, "Mom was Spanish and my father Norwegian. Just call me 'Bo'!"

Tyler and Rabbit headed for the kitchen. The next few hours were a blur. In the large kitchen, Tyler joined volunteers, and men, women and older children who lived at the shelter to prepare and serve breakfast to over two hundred people. He cooked, washed dishes and cooked some more. About noon they finished the second seating, cleaned the kitchen and dining hall tables. Rabbit told Tyler other volunteers and residents would prepare and serve the evening meal.

The final job was to take out the garbage to the large containers in the alley. Tyler paused when he returned to see if there was anything else. All of the other volunteers had left. Rabbit and Bo Peterson were nowhere to be seen. His eyes came to rest on an old man standing in the far corner cutting another man's hair. The barber had silver hair, a neatly trimmed mustache and surprisingly wore dark blue pants and a matching vest over a white shirt and tie. Tyler studied the scene. The barber's suit jacket was on a hanger near by. His customer occasionally laughed and grinned. He was obviously listening to the old man. The scissors flashed and hair rained.

"Want your ears lowered?" Rabbit had come up behind Tyler. "That's Scissors our barber. He's here most of the time. We've become good friends. When he is not cutting hair, he is usually listening to people. He's a great listener. Most of the adults here think of him as a wise uncle or even father. Of course, to the children, he is a grandfather who cuts hair and usually has candy for his grandchildren. He gives a very professional haircut. Even Bo and the Collector have him cut their hair. He won't take a dime from anyone. He cuts the ladies' hair too. He's a nice old man and likes to be called Scissors. Now, if you have time, how about a tour of the shelter?"

"Great! Lead on," Tyler replied.

On the second and third floors, Rabbit showed Tyler large rooms which served as dormitories. At the end of each bed was a footlocker for people who would be returning at night. The children slept with their mothers in smaller rooms. There were only a few bathrooms. According to Rabbit, the shelter needed renovations. He told Tyler every person who stayed overnight had responsibilities regarding keeping their area and room clean, making their beds and washing their clothes and the bed linen.

Back on the main floor, Rabbit opened a door to a room, which served as a lounge, study area and conference place for social workers, volunteer nurses, lawyers and residents. In addition, there was one good size room where Bo Peterson could meet with small groups of people or his staff.

"Well, that's about it, my friend," Rabbit concluded. "T'ain't much, but it's home for many of us lucky ones. There are over three thousand homeless in this city. There are beds for less than two thousand. As you saw, there are a lot of young mothers with children. I hate to think of where they sleep if they can't find a space in a shelter. Bo said the volunteer advisory board has an option on a parcel of land nearby, but until they can find big bucks, another shelter is just a dream."

"Bo runs a tight ship. No second chances. Anybody who gets mean, does drugs or is light fingered leaves immediately. Anybody who has a problem with leaving discusses it with the Collector. He listens, provides suggestions where personal help can be found but then the person leaves quietly. The Collector is a very bright, compassionate but tough man. He'll never tell you but he has PhD's in psychology and philosophy. If it weren't for him, I wouldn't be alive, but that's another story."

They returned to the dining room where the Collector was sitting in his wheelchair near the exit door talking with the director.

"You're a good man, Rabbit," the director said. "I knew Tyler was in good hands. Will you be back in a couple of weeks, Tyler?"

"Yes, I certainly will," Tyler responded.

The director continued, "Tyler, we exist because companies and individuals donate food, volunteers give their time and our board raises money. We would like to help people with drug and alcohol dependencies, shelter more women and children and feed more people, but our space and resources are limited. Maybe someday we will be able to expand or even build another shelter. We appreciate your joining us. You did a good job. I could see everyone liked the quiet, friendly way you went about your work and served the food. Thanks again for coming."

"Which way are you going, Tyler?" the Collector asked.

"I'll take the blue bus back to Hamilton," he replied.

"Well, I am heading back to where I live. There is a bus stop for Hamilton right across the street. Do you want to walk and talk a bit?" the Collector queried.

"Sure, and I would be happy to push," Tyler offered.

Rabbit, Bo and the Collector roared with laughter. Tyler flushed.

Bo, still chuckling, spoke, "Tyler, you meant well and I know the Collector appreciated your offer but if you, Rabbit and I combined our strength, we would still lose an arm wrestling match to the Collector. He bench presses over three-hundred pounds and has won wheelchair races, including marathons, across the country. If he is ever upset with you, don't let him shake your hand."

Everyone laughed. Tyler got the message. He held the door as the Collector wheeled through. It was a crisp, blinding bright Fall afternoon. The sun reflected off a shiny yellow taxi that waited at the curb.

"Bones, don't tell me it's Monday already?" the Collector asked the tall, thin man leaning against the cab.

"Hi, Collector. No, you're right as usual," the man answered with a grin. "You certainly know your days of the week. How you remember all those complicated facts is beyond this old head. The truth is, I just dropped off a fare in the neighborhood, and I thought you might like to go for a joy ride for a change."

The Collector wheeled to his friend. They warmly shook hands. "Thanks, Bones," the Collector said. "Appreciate your thinking of me, but I'm still on duty. I'm bringing lunch to the two other Congress Street Musketeers. I will need you Monday as always. I haven't been to the north side for two weeks. Before you go, Bones, meet a new friend, Tyler Smith. He knows how to work."

Bones took one long step and held out his hand. "Nice to meet you, Tyler," Bones said, looking him in the eyes. "The Collector's a good friend to have. My only advice is don't stand in front of the Collector's wheelchair. That could be dangerous. Take care, gentlemen—Monday, Collector."

A few moments later, the taxi was gone. The Collector didn't look up as he spoke. "Tyler, you just met one fine man. His real name is Wilson Garth, but since boot camp he has been Bones. He is my oldest friend and drives me wherever I need to go. Let's get moving."

"Tell me about yourself, Tyler, your family, your interests, your dreams and your social life, if it's not a state secret?" the Collector asked with a grin.

Tyler started with his high school courses, then he jumped back to his birth, unknown parents, his adopted family, the accident, his computer, sports and, finally, Habitat and Maria. Tyler felt comfortable sharing his life with his new friend and this surprised him. Tyler mentioned his fascination with reading about the lives of inventors and the spiritual leaders of history, but admitted he wasn't sure where this interest was leading him. The Collector listened in silence.

"That's it, Collector," Tyler said smiling. "I've got a lot to learn. Now, I'd like to learn what you are willing to share of your life."

"Touché!" the Collector agreed. "I think that's fair, but since I'm three times your age, I will just hit the high and low spots. If I don't, we will walk across the state line before I am finished."

The Collector said he, too, had been lucky. He had good parents, and was a good enough high school athlete to get a partial scholarship to college for football and baseball. When he graduated from the university, the Vietnam War was at its height. He enlisted. In Vietnam, he saw friends and enemy soldiers die. During one firefight, he was wounded and captured. Viet Cong doctors saved his life by amputating his feet. He spent three years in prison before being repatriated.

According to the Collector, he learned a lot in the military. Early in basic training, three guys decided they didn't like his background. They had come from a community far different from the one the Collector had known. A tall, wiry kid, who knew the threesome, came and stood beside the Collector. The stranger didn't say anything but his face sent a message. The three guys left. The tall, wiry kid was Bones. He and the Collector became best friends. They went to Vietnam and watched out for each other in the jungle, rice paddies and deltas. Together,

they survived. Together, they saw human beings at their worst and at their best.

"In prison camp," the Collector related, "I had lots of time to think and wonder. In my cell, my only friends were mice and spiders. They were good teachers. They live in their own separate worlds but occasionally those worlds would collide.

"The mouse would run through the spider's web and the cobwebs would affect the vision of the mouse. Their worlds were upset for a short time. Once in awhile, I was allowed outside to sit near the prison fence. There I watched other worlds—the worlds of flowers and butterflies, to name just two. They intentionally share their worlds.

"Like the butterfly or bee, human beings have the opportunity to interact with other worlds. Each person lives in his own world but when two people meet each other, their world is changed. In some way, good or bad, we change the life of every person we meet, and they change us. I am not the same person I was before I met you, Tyler. Possibly, you, too, are a little different because of our meeting.

"We know each human is unique. All living organisms must adapt to their singular world in order to survive. Some human worlds are much tougher than others. Often, I wondered why some children are born with illnesses and others with good health, some with limited intelligence and others are very bright, some in a harsh environment and others in a nurturing land, some to parents who find it hard to love or others to loving parents. No one, I know, can answer any of those questions.

"I came to believe the purpose of our existence is twofold. One, to complete our own spiritual journey, and, two, to support others who are making the same trip. We are asked to do our best with the abilities we have been given wherever we live. We can make someone else's life a little bit better—maybe even a lot better. We are here to make a difference. In prison, I tried to focus on the spiritual aspect of my life. It kept me alive. I returned to the United States and the university to better prepare to work with people who are fighting their own personal battles. What I am doing is meaningful for me."

Tyler was moved and impressed with the Collector's openness and dedication. He asked, "One question? Can you tell me how you got the name, Collector?"

"That's easy, my friend. I collect information and sometimes people. During my first year working on the street, I was amazed how many people did not know where shelters were, where they could get a meal, or where there were programs which might help them. I met veterans who served their country, lived on the street and who didn't know medical and financial assistance was available. There are individuals who were employed many years and are eligible for social security but do not know how or where to apply for it. Sometimes I just tell folks. Sometimes I have to take them gently by the hand.

"Thanks to Bones, I am able to travel all over our city collecting and sharing information. Most homeless people don't mind telling me their names or giving me a little personal information. Once in a while someone comes to Mencius House looking for a family member. My list occasionally allows us to reunite a family, and that is a wonderful event to see. My information assists social workers, doctors and even lawyers that are assisting homeless people. I wish the information was available to more people.

"I don't use a three ring notebook. If you looked into that pack strapped to my wheelchair, you would see the latest Micron Laptop computer. There are hundreds of "Collectors" across the U.S. We e-mail each other, evaluating the programs for the homeless in our respective cities and towns. Many cities have a web site for the homeless. We need one here in Merrelburg. Maybe we can talk more about that possibility? Well, Tyler we are almost home. My apartment is two blocks away, but most nights I sleep here."

Tyler didn't see "here." He saw only office buildings and the large opening to the Congress Street subway station. The Collector wheeled across the street to the gaping mouth of the station. Tyler followed. They descended two levels in an elevator. The air became musty and damp. Around a bend and before the turnstiles was an alcove with several supermarket carts. An orange tarpaulin was draped over them.

"Nous sommes arrivee!" The Collector exclaimed as he rolled up to the pushcarts. "Ahoy there, Bottleman and Cat Lady! It's the Collector. I've got supper and a friend."

All was quiet behind the circled wagons. The first sound Tyler heard was the meowing of a cat. A curious feline pushed its face between pieces of the hanging tarpaulin. Rustling sounds followed and the top of a red wool cap appeared. Under it there was the slightly dirty, tired face of a woman. She was wrapped in a ragged heavy brown coat and held tightly to another cat. She seemed to acknowledge the Collector's presence but wouldn't raise her eyes.

"Good afternoon, Cat Lady," the Collector began. "You look fine. I brought you some sandwiches and soup from Mencius House."

A pair of scruffy wool gloves covered the Cat Lady's hands. She slowly put forward one hand and retrieved her meal without a word and disappeared behind her carts. She never looked up.

The Collector moved to a small opening in the cart wall and went inside. A poorly dressed man lay on layers of cardboard. He was wrapped in a ragged blanket. His face had no color. Sunken cheeks and hollowed eyes made him appear old. He found the strength to give the Collector a smile. Tyler did not know what to say.

"It's okay, Bottleman, I'm here," the Collector assured his friend. "I've got medicine and some soup. How about sitting up a bit if we help you?" The Bottleman slowly nodded.

The Collector and Tyler carefully raised the Bottleman. Tyler held him while the Collector spoon-fed him soup and gave him some pills. Tyler looked at the red Nike baseball cap the man wore and the Silver Star pinned on it. Tyler didn't say anything. The Bottleman had a hard time swallowing without coughing but managed a number of spoonfuls. When he had had enough, they lowered him to an old pillow.

"Thanks a lot," he whispered looking at both the Collector and Tyler and then he closed his eyes. Standing up, Tyler glanced at the now sleeping man and at the huddled lady sitting a few feet away, stroking her two cats as she fed them part of her sandwich. How does this happen in America? This was just one of the questions Tyler was asking himself.

"Let's see if the sun's gone down," the Collector suggested, and they took the elevator to the street level. Without waiting for Tyler's questions, the Collector spoke, "Most nights I sleep here. My two friends are defenseless, although they have nothing anyone would want to steal. The police in this district know me. They don't bother us and even seem to care how we are doing. The city government, like the average person, has mixed feelings toward the homeless. They feel sorry for them and, at the same time, would like them to vanish. I'm afraid that won't happen in the near future.

"The Bottleman was practically born on the streets. His father beat him, and he ran away from his home before he was thirteen. Churches and missions kept him safe at night and showed him another side of human nature. He learned to read and survived by walking many miles each day searching for bottles and cans to turn in for money and books. The money supplied his basic needs. Any extra he spent buying food and things for others. Even tough guys never bothered him—the word on the street was that he is a very gentle human being. He knows he has an incurable disease. He never complains. He does not want to stay in a shelter or go to a hospital, but soon we will have to take him to a hospice center.

"The Cat Lady lives in her own mental world. Whether or not she will ever return to our world is impossible to say. Something terrible must have happened in her life that she does not want to remember. I think she may have had a family. She lovingly takes care of her cats and keeps herself as clean and neat as possible. I'll continue to do what I can for her. On the street, it's one day at a time.

"Speaking of days, Tyler, you've had a long day. I've enjoyed your company. Thanks for the help. We will talk more the next time we meet." Tyler nodded, smiled and shook the Collector's hand before darting across the street to the bus stop.

Tyler stared out the bus window. He thought of all he had experienced in one short day. Like a traveler on a tour, he had been shown a different world—a poor country whose beauty was only in the eyes and souls of its people. He imagined there were thousands of worlds, just like the one he saw in Merrelburg, in almost all the cities on the planet. All could easily be discovered but were mostly avoided.

Chapter VI

At supper that night, Tyler related his day to his parents. He convinced his father to think about donating some time at Mencius House. Tyler's parents were impressed with the depth of their son's concern. Since the accident, he had worn his heart on his sleeve.

The next week, following his T'ai Chi class, Tyler and Maria talked at length about the homeless. She thought there might be something she and her friends could do, but she didn't say more. When he returned home, he accessed the internet to search for information on Vietnam and the homeless. He was amazed to find there were hundreds of web sites about the homeless which contained information written by a diverse group of people; clergy, social workers, shelter administrators, lawyers, government officials, economists and even some obviously very bright homeless individuals. It was a huge problem nationally and internationally and getting worse.

Tyler decided to return to the shelter whenever he could. A few days later, he learned his dad had contacted the clinic which served the residents of shelters. They were pleased his father was willing to see people at Mencius House once a month. The following Saturday, Tyler and his dad left their home early for the city.

Tyler introduced his dad to Bo and then went right to work in the kitchen. He didn't see his father again until after the second serving of breakfast. Late in the morning a man tapped Tyler on the shoulder. "Excuse me, Sir," his father said, grinning. "Could I have a second cup of coffee—I sure could use one. Tyler, I expect to be here all day. If you decide to go home before I am through, let me know. See you."

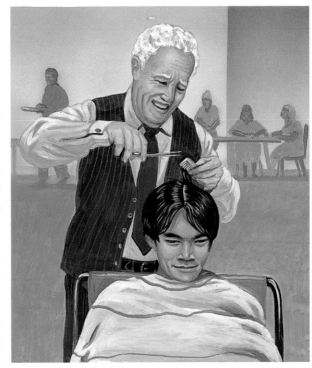

Tyler smiled. He knew his dad probably would be leaving late. When he finished wiping off the last table, he returned to the kitchen to speak with Donna. Donna had been volunteering at Mencius House for years. She ruled the kitchen as a benevolent queen. Tyler asked about getting some food for his dad. A few minutes later, he was carrying a full plate of scrambled eggs, bacon and toast. A quick knock, an opened door, a surprised look from an appreciative father and Tyler was gone. He had promised Donna to return later to cut up vegetables for the supper's chicken soup.

Tyler noticed Scissors was by himself and he walked in his direction. *"Buon Giorno,"* was the total of Tyler's Italian, but he let it fly.

The old man broke out into a big grin. *"Buon Giorno!"* How are you?" Scissors replied. "Sit down, my young friend. You're a hard worker, but you need a trim and my price is right."

A little apprehensive, Tyler sat down on a kitchen chair. Scissors threw a clean white towel around Tyler's shoulders and tucked it under his chin. With the first snip, came the first question. While his hair cascaded to the floor, Tyler answered questions. When Scissors was finished, he handed Tyler a mirror and held a second mirror behind Tyler's head. Tyler knew it was probably the best haircut he had ever had and he told Scissors so. The old barber beamed. He had learned a lot about Tyler's life. Tyler had learned little about Scissors. Tyler took out his wallet.

"I'm glad you like it," Scissors replied smiling. "But I can't accept money. Tyler, like you, I enjoy giving what I can. I'll see you, same chair, in a couple of weeks. I see I have more customers."

Two little girls had been sitting patiently at the next table watching. Each received a hug from the old man and, in return, he received a kiss on a cheek. The smallest child was lifted onto the kitchen chair. Tyler shook Scissors's hand and patted him on the back. He wondered how many guys get their hair cut by a barber with a three-piece suit.

"Yo, Tyler," the Collector called, "Got a minute?" Tyler walked to the far end of the dinning room and joined his friend at a table.

"I see you've received a 'Scissors Special,'" observed the Collector. "Looks good. He knows his business—if that was his business. Scissors is a mystery to us, but he may be just like thousands in the United States. One missed paycheck, an illness that uses up all their savings or a family financial disaster, and they are on the street, sleeping in a car, under a bridge or, if lucky, in a shelter. The fortunate ones get help finding a job, locating housing and slowly get back on their feet. All we know about Scissors is he likes people, likes to cut hair and may be poor but not penniless. He sits with different individuals and families at mealtime and stays the night when we have an extra bed. Everyone loves him—no one knows where he goes when he is not here.

"This brings me to my question of the day. Stored in my computer is data on all the shelters, clinics, social services and volunteers who work with the homeless in our city. I also have short biographies on hundreds of homeless people who have volunteered information in case a relative ever wishes to find them. We do not have a web site. Collectors like me, across our state, with a web site could exchange information much more rapidly and reach thousands who have an interest in helping the homeless. Tyler, we have no money to create or maintain a web site and I wondered if you had any ideas?"

Tyler's mind had been nanoseconds ahead of the Collector. Several possibilities for accomplishing the Collector's project swirled in his mind. "I'll give it my best shot, Collector," Tyler replied. "I think it's possible. Next week, I'll bring in a zip drive so you can download your data."

Back in the kitchen, as promised, Tyler joined other volunteers cutting up vegetables and taking the meat off a dozen chickens that had been boiled. Later, he unloaded vans that brought donated food from stores and near-by restaurants. By the time supper was ready to be served, over one hundred people had gathered, and more were waiting outside the shelter. Tyler had put in a full day, but he still wasn't finished. His dad finally appeared and joined a family at a table.

Tyler watched him. In a few minutes, his father was chatting easily with the lady and her children along with enjoying a bowl of chicken soup and French bread. Tyler was proud of his dad. He seemed very much at home.

An hour later, Tyler and his dad were on their way home to Hamilton, sharing tales about their day's work. Tyler's father described the different levels of health he had found among the people at the shelter. Some adults were in great shape, but others and many of the children needed to be treated by doctors at the clinic. He had given a list to Bo who had promised to meet with the social worker and arrange transportation. Tyler's dad was very concerned about the children—some were undernourished, others had sores and colds that needed to be treated and watched closely. He shook his head and sighed. He knew many of the people would be some-place else in a few days.

In the week that followed, Tyler almost gave up sleeping. On Monday after school, he asked his friend, Jason Goldman, if he could arrange a special meeting of the computer club. Jason, who was now president of the club, got the word out. After school, Tyler described the purpose of Mencius House, his work and the Collector's and the need for a web site to a full house. Without exception, the club's advisor and the members thought it would be a fun and worth-while project. They would begin designing a web site as soon as Tyler brought them the data.

That evening Tyler went to Computer World and met with Mr. Donabedian, the owner. He related his experiences at the shelter, their many needs and how being on the internet would help. Mr. Donabedian listened carefully, asked some difficult questions and finally said he would be happy to do what he could. He gave Tyler a zip drive and offered to supply used computers for teaching. Tyler had to come up with the teachers. Tyler smiled as he thought—one challenge accomplished, another challenge proposed. He thanked Mr. Donabedian profusely.

Tyler knew the Collector always went online after breakfast at Mencius House. Before he left for school, he e-mailed the Collector asking him for a meeting in the afternoon. A few minutes later, Tyler opened his e-mail to find a note from the Collector suggesting Congress Street Station at 4:00 p.m.

Tyler stepped off the bus just before 4:00 p.m. and walked down into the station. He was just one of hundreds of people hurrying in and out of the subway. He slowed as he approached the tarpaulin covered pushcart corral. Above the sounds of the rushing shoes, he heard the Collector's voice talking softly to the Bottleman, "Please, just a couple more spoonfuls."

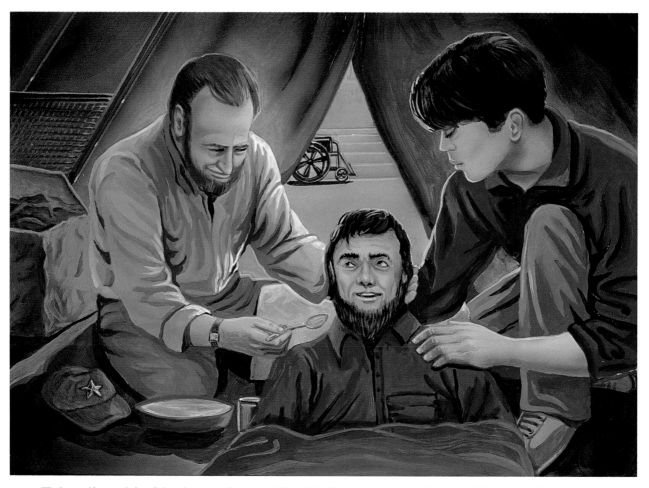

Tyler slipped inside the enclosure. The Collector was sitting holding the Bottleman with his left hand as he gently directed a spoonful into his friend's mouth. Tyler knelt down beside the ill man and held his shoulder, prompting him to raise his eyes for an instant and give Tyler a weak smile. "That's all—good job," the Collector said, and he and Tyler slowly lowered the sick man. The Bottleman's eyes closed immediately.

As the Collector busied himself cleaning up around the Bottleman and trying to make him comfortable, Tyler looked over at the Cat Lady. She was stroking one of her cats while the other licked the bottom of an empty plastic food container. She seemed not to be aware that the Collector and the Bottleman were only a few feet away. Tyler crawled toward the cat that had finished eating. Slowly, he reached out his hand to pat the cat. After one soft touch, the cat began to purr and moved over to rub against Tyler. His new friend crawled into his lap. Side by side in silence, Tyler and the Cat Lady stroked their feline friends. Maybe she felt Tyler's presence but her eyes remained fixed on the cat in her lap.

Finally, the Collector whispered, "Let's go." The Collector crawled to his wheelchair, hoisted himself up and, without another word, led Tyler to the street. Outside they waited for the light to change. Then the Collector targeted the front doors of the First Union National Bank. The automatic doors swung open.

A well-dressed man behind an imposing desk jumped up to meet the duo a few feet inside the door.

"Welcome, Collector," he said. "Great to see you. Got some banking business today?" The two warmly shook hands. "Thanks, Tyrone," the Collector replied. "Always good to see you. Today I just need a quiet spot, an electrical outlet and a phone. Shake hands with a good friend who helps out at Mencius House, Tyler Smith."

Tyler looked up at a gigantic man with an equally large smile. He wondered if he would get his hand back in one piece. The big man's grip was firm but gentle. After telling Tyler that any friend of the Collector's was his for life, they followed him to a private room.

Alone, the Collector spoke, "Tyler, that big man has an even bigger heart. He played pro-football and could have spent his private life in a wealthy gated community but decided to return to where he grew up to try to give the youngsters struggling in his old neighborhood a better chance. He's doing it. Now, here's my computer. I think you better handle the transfer and I will review the files with you so you won't be bothered with extraneous information."

Two hours later, all the appropriate files had been transferred to the zip drive. The Collector gave Tyler written notes telling the history of the shelter and a few paragraphs written by Bo Peterson, residents, volunteers, and others connected with Mencius House. On the bus, Tyler began to mentally envision and organize the shelter's home page.

At the computer club's meeting the next day, Tyler outlined his rough ideas on Mencius House's web site to Jason and the other members of the club. They had a few questions but were eager to begin the project. They would download the data that day and begin organizing tomorrow. Tyler should have the first draft for the Collector by the end of the week. After thanking everyone, Tyler headed for home to study for a couple of hours before T'ai Chi.

Maria met Tyler in the evening at the class. Tyler was dressed for the session but had barely time to greet his friend or her mother. By the end of the hour-and-a-half, everyone, young and old, wondered if they ever would achieve the grace and fluid movement of Yoshi. It had been a strenuous, yet relaxing workout. It was time for a little nourishment.

Tyler gave the waiter the order. In a few minutes he had brought Maria up-to-date on his experiences at Mencius House and its many needs. He told of the gift of computers they had received along with his responsibility to find teachers. Tyler's second concern was finding someone willing to pay the yearly costs of a server allowing Mencius House to connect to the internet. Tyler wondered out loud if it would all come together.

"Sometimes when we look at all the problems of a project," Maria began, "the goal appears to be overwhelming. Mom is forever repeating the Chinese proverb: 'A thousand mile journey begins with a single step.' I thought the shelter might need tutors so a few days ago, I spoke with members of our school's National Honor Society. The members said they would be happy to provide tutors with or without computers two days per week. They are scouting around for all levels of books to use as well as getting book donations to create a small library for the shelter. As to where you will find money for the server, I haven't a clue, but I bet it will happen."

"Thanks, Maria—as always—you were a step ahead of me. Terrific!" Tyler exclaimed. "You, your volunteers and donations will make a difference. Maybe our honor society would be willing to do the same thing. My skills at the moment seem to be washing dishes, chopping vegetables and deboning chickens. Someday I'll make a great wife."

Maria laughed and changed the conversation to less serious subjects: specifically, their Saturday night date and the month's two Junior Proms. Tyler was lucky. He was now just about the same size as his dad, so he had only to look as far as his father's closet for his tux. Maria wanted a dress which would be appropriate for dances, weddings and special occasions. Her Aunt Mishico was an accomplished seamstress and had offered to design and make Maria's dress. They finished their food and returned to the studio just as Maria's mother was completing her meditation.

Sleepily, Tyler climbed aboard the Saturday morning bus. He went right to sleep but the driver recognized Tyler and stopped at the shelter. "Have a good day, Tyler," he called. Tyler was anxious to give the Collector the rough draft of the Mencius House's web site his class-mates had created. He thought they had done a fine job and hoped the Collector would be pleased. The Collector was not only pleased but also thrilled with the professional look of the web site. He had a few suggestions and information he had forgotten to include, but for all practical purposes the site was done.

"Thanks for the gifts from your friend at Computer World and the work of your computer club. We are well on our way," the Collector commented. "Now all we need is someone to sponsor our server. We will find one, I know. Oh, I wanted to tell you, the Bottleman is not very well. Bones and I are going to see him this afternoon. Would you come? It would mean a lot to the Bottleman. The way you treated him—touched him. He considers you one of his few friends."

"He touched me, too," Tyler replied. "Yes, I will be happy to go with you, but now I'd better get moving before Donna fires me. See you later."

The Collector wheeled in another direction as Tyler headed for the kitchen. On the way, he paused to greet Scissors who was sweeping up hair from previous customers. He was humming *Un belle dia* from Madame Butterfly. Tyler only knew it sounded nice. A rather disheveled lady was waiting for Scissors, so he and Tyler simply swapped "Ciaio's" and smiles. As always, Tyler was so busy serving, cooking and washing that the hours flew by. While he and Rabbit were washing the tables, Tyler told him of the Bottleman's condition. Rabbit sadly nodded.

Tyler asked Rabbit a question, "I saw a Silver Star pinned to the Bottleman's cap. Was he in the war like the Collector?"

Rabbit smiled, "No, the Bottleman wasn't in the service. The Silver Star is one of the Collector's military decorations. During a firefight, the Collector saved a number of his men's lives including Bones. Even though a machine gun chewed up his legs, he held his position so his buddies could get away. He was closer to being dead than alive when the Viet Cong found him. Vietnamese doctors saved his life even though he lost his feet. He never says a bad word about the enemy or talks about the war. In fact, he never says a mean or bad word about anyone. When he gave the Silver Star to the Bottleman, he told him he deserved it because of the way he has courageously lived his life. The Bottleman knows the star will be buried with him. Please don't mention I told you. The Collector might run me over with that tank-wheelchair he drives."

Tyler promised.

The Collector was waiting near the door. Tyler buttoned his coat. Fall was coming to a close. Outside, Bones was waiting. After the Collector slid into the front seat of the taxi, Bones closed up the wheelchair and fastened it to the special rack on the car's trunk. Tyler got in the backseat. The three didn't say much as they drove. At the hospice center, they were taken directly to the Bottleman's room.

The Bottleman lay motionless on clean white sheets—his eyes were closed. Four street people sat silently on chairs. The Bottleman's red cap with the shining Silver Star lay on his chest. The Collector rolled his wheelchair to the side of the bed and took the Bottleman's hand. Tyler and Bones stood behind the Collector.

In a firm yet gentle voice, the Collector spoke, "Bottleman, friends are here. Can you open your eyes? We love you!"

Slowly, the Bottleman opened his eyes. It took a long time and obvious great effort for him to focus on everyone surrounding his bed. A tear rolled down his cheek and then he whispered, "I love you, too." Slowly, very slowly he made eye contact with each person and then closed his eyes.

Bones took the Collector and Tyler to Congress Street station. It was a quiet trip as each man kept his own thoughts. When they arrived, Bones reviewed the Collector's transportation needs for the next week. He then lightened the mood by telling them he was off to a family reunion and their annual softball game. The Collector told Bones to remember his advanced age, as good chauffeurs were hard to find. They all laughed. Outside the cab, friends greeted the Collector as he and Tyler entered the station.

They found the Cat Lady, as usual, petting her cats. The Collector gave her food. Tyler knelt down beside her and stroked one of the cats. The Cat Lady didn't move away. Slowly her hand moved to her side and reached for something. Without raising her head, she held out a metal flashlight to Tyler. When he did not immediately take it, the Cat Lady raised and turned her head. She looked into Tyler's eyes. For a moment, she seemed to be in the same world as Tyler. She spoke a single word, "Please."

Tyler took the flashlight from the Cat Lady's hand. Instantly, her head dropped and her hands clasped her cats. Tyler smiled, nodded and stood up. The Collector had been watching, "Jeez," he whispered. "That's the first word I ever heard the Cat Lady speak. I think that old flashlight is the only thing she owns from her previous life. Do you think you can fix it?"

"Well," Tyler replied. "Let's have a look."

Tyler began examining the dirty, tarnished flashlight. It had been of good quality when new but now was rusty. It took considerable strength for Tyler to unscrew the back. Looking inside he saw there were no batteries, the wires were corroded and the bulb obviously burnt out. He found the switch was stuck fast and the glass lens cover was badly cracked.

"It would be a lot easier to buy a new one than try and repair that flashlight, Tyler," the Collector observed. "What are you going to do?"

"You're right," Tyler responded. "but it seems this flashlight is very special to the Cat Lady. Our friend wants me to fix it. I'll try. If it is possible to repair, I will bring it back tomorrow. Right now, I'd better go home. Monday, I'll pass on your corrections and additions to Jason and his crew. I expect you will have the final version by the end of the week. I'll see you then—take care."

Tyler and the Collector shook hands. Tyler's bus pulled into Congress Street a few minutes later.

That night, Tyler sat at his workbench for over two hours repairing the flashlight. First he took it completely apart and then began thoroughly cleaning each piece. He removed all the rust, replaced the wires, the bulb, installed a new switch, added batteries and a new lens cover. He pushed the top switch. There was light. Tyler smiled. With a fresh cloth he began removing the grime from the heavy metal silver shell. Underneath one patch of dirt, scratched neatly in the metal were the words, "To Mom with love, Barbara, Frank and Tim." Tyler paused and wondered how important this inscription had been to the Cat Lady.

True to his word, Sunday after church, Tyler returned to the city and Congress Street Station. As he approached the pushcart enclosure, he heard the meowing of the cats. The Cat Lady sat alone petting one of her friends. She didn't appear to hear Tyler's footsteps, but when he knelt down beside her and he turned on the flashlight, the Cat Lady reacted. She turned and looked directly at Tyler. She accepted the flashlight from him and smiled. Tyler nodded, touched her very gently on a shoulder, smiled and quietly left to return to Hamilton. The Cat Lady switched the flashlight on and off. She smiled again, stood up and began to organize her things.

After getting dressed Monday, Tyler followed his daily routine turning on "Gates" and checking his e-mail. Maria had written him a long letter telling Tyler how she and two other girls had enjoyed tutoring children at the Shelter on Saturday. She then went on to describe the progress her aunt was making on her prom dress. There were several letters from Jason and other classmates. Jason mentioned the Mencius House web site team had a little surprise in store for him. The final e-mail was from the Collector. It puzzled and worried him.

"Hi, Partner," the Collector had written. "Hope all is well. By any chance did you fix that flashlight and return it Sunday to the Cat Lady? I returned late Sunday evening and found her gone. Everything she owned was missing as well as one pushcart. I assume something or someone made her leave. None of the street people in the area have seen her. Any ideas? C."

Tyler read the Collector's letter twice before sitting down at his computer. In his e-mail, he mentioned he had been able to fix the light and saw the Cat Lady early Sunday afternoon. Tyler described how the Cat Lady made eye contact when she received the flashlight, even smiled, but she hadn't said a word. He reported he left directly and hoped the Cat Lady was safe.

That afternoon, Tyler met with Jason and the computer club. He returned the copy of Mencius House's web site along with the additions and corrections from the Collector. It took a few minutes to discuss the changes, new pictures and the final format. Tyler personally thanked every student for all the work they had done and told them how much the Collector appreciated their efforts and looked forward to meeting them someday at Mencius House.

Jason Goldman rose and looking directly at Tyler, raised his hands as his fingers rapidly changed positions. Another friend stood at his side, verbally interpreting Jason's signing so members of the club who could not read sign language would understand what Jason was saying. "Tyler, before you leave and we get to work," Jason signed, "and unless things changed over the weekend, you still need funding for this web site. Right?"

Tyler nodded, "That still is the situation."

Jason continued, "We sent an ad hoc committee to meet with our principal last week regarding Mencius House and our project. To make a long story short, the Student Council met the next day and discussed our proposal. On Friday, the students and faculty of Hamilton High voted to make a multi-year commitment to Mencius House to pay for maintaining a web site and for the Server. You will also be hearing from juniors and seniors that would like to volunteer."

Tyler was momentarily speechless. Then he took a few moments to share some of the things he had learned at the shelter and thanked everyone again.

Tyler's life slowed down a bit. The Collector was thrilled with the web site, the number of hits it was receiving, and with the volunteers from Tyler's school who were acting as cyberspace secretaries for the Collector. The only disturbing news was the Cat Lady seemed to have vanished from the city. Maria and Tyler were ready for the proms. Tyler continued to meet with the Collector and worked at the shelter on Saturdays. Early afternoon on a prom Saturday, Tyler was receiving a trim from Scissors.

"What color flowers did you buy for our beautiful Maria?" Scissors asked. "Don't move—just talk!"

Tyler kept his head still but moved his lips. "How do baby white orchids sound with a touch of blue that complements her dress?"

"Molto bene! Molto bene!" Scissors commented as he whipped the towel from under Tyler's chin.

"Now you are a Prince Charming!"

"Thanks, Scissors," Tyler responded. "I have another favor to ask. You have met Dad, and you know Maria and me well. We all want you to have Thanksgiving with us. My folks told me not to take 'no' for an answer. Mom wants to know if there is anything you don't like or can't eat. She and Sarah will make your favorite dessert. Sarah is my eleven year old little sister. You'll love her. We will pick you up about 9:00 a.m., Thursday morning. Please say yes."

The small old man held his towel in both hands. A melancholy look and then a smile appeared on his face. "I had a Sarah in my life many years ago, too. Yes, Tyler, I will be delighted, and please thank your family for me. I accept. As far as food is concerned, I can eat anything and dream of homemade apple pies."

"Great!" exclaimed Tyler. "Maria and I will pick you up here at Mencius House. By the way, you are in luck. Mom makes the best apple pies in the world and I select the best ice cream to go on top of it."

Scissors and Tyler hugged. They went their separate ways with the old man looking forward to a family Thanksgiving and the young man thinking how nice it will be for Maria's and Tyler's families to share Thanksgiving with Scissors.

The Hamilton High School prom was perfect. Maria looked lovely. An Indian summer night with a clear sky full of twinkling stars made it magic. The theme was the year 3000. The gym was decorated with space ships and extra-terrestrial creatures. An "OUT OF THIS WORLD" disk jockey and an alien musical group kept the music ricocheting off the walls. Tyler's and Maria's parents were members of the chaperone contingent but their SciFi costumes disguised their identities. Green Cheese, Solar System Sodas, Galaxy Goopers and other weird-named edibles and planetary drinks fit right in. The cheerleaders introduced a new dance, the Galactic Gyro. It was a lot of fun and laughs.

The following Thursday, Tyler and Maria drove to Merrelburg to collect Scissors. Inside Mencius House, sitting near the door, was a distinguished looking old man in a cleaned and pressed three-piece navy blue suit. He wore a freshly laundered white shirt and polished black shoes. Scissors held a newspaper-wrapped package in his lap along with a dark overcoat, a fedora and gloves. He stood up when Tyler opened the door. The two shook hands and embraced.

Maria opened up the rear door of the car as Scissors and Tyler approached. "Gee, Tyler," Maria began, "I think if I had met this handsome gentleman before the prom you might have had to look for another date. You look very dashing, Scissors. I'm glad to see you brought a topcoat. It's going to be nippy until the sun climbs higher. We wondered if you would like to go to the Thanksgiving Day football game at Tyler's school, or would you like to go directly to the Smiths?"

"When I was much younger," Scissors responded, "we would go to some sporting event, if we weren't playing ourselves, almost every week. I'd love to go."

Maria had brought along extra seat cushions, blankets, muffins and a thermos of hot chocolate. One of her hobbies was photography. As soon as they arrived at the stadium, she began taking pictures of Scissors, Tyler and the game. The bleachers were full of students and parents, and colorful banners waved in tune with the schools' bands. It turned out to be an exciting game. Scissors knew his football and asked good questions about Tyler's team and its players.

The final whistle blew just before noon.

A short drive and the threesome were walking up the front path to Tyler's home. Sarah had been watching out the window with Marley, the family's black and tan cocker spaniel. They rushed to the front door as soon as the family car came in sight. Sarah and Marley ran past Tyler and Maria, and Sarah lassoed the old man with open arms. Marley welcomed him with gentle woofs. Scissors bent over and returned her warm embrace. Maria caught them on camera.

"Welcome, Grandpa Scissors," Sarah cried. "Marley and I have been looking forward to your visit. We've been looking out that window all morning. Is it okay to call you, Grandpa? I really could use another Grandpa."

Scissors grinned, "Sarah, it is nice to meet you. I have heard a lot of nice things about you from your brother. It would make me very happy if you would call me Grandpa."

Sarah beamed, then greeted Maria and Tyler. Sarah escorted Scissors into the house. In the living room, Scissors met the rest of the family and guests including Maria's parents and her two brothers. Sarah was anxious to take Scissors on a tour.

Scissors whispered to Sarah, "Would you and Anthony help me open this package before we go and see the rest of the house?"

Children love to open packages, and Sarah and Anthony were not exceptions. Carefully they helped Scissors remove the many layers of papers. Inside the package were beautiful, fresh long stemmed red roses with flakes of gold on each petal. They were breathtaking. Scissors passed one out to each of the ladies. He had not forgotten anyone. Sarah went with her mother to find vases for the flowers. When they were arranged the women wanted to know where Scissors had gotten such beautiful roses, but he would say no more than "a friend."

It proved to be a delightful Thanksgiving for all. Before dinner, Scissors got the grand tour thanks to Sarah, Anthony and Marley. The turkey dinner and all the fixings were delicious. There was only one awkward moment. The adults had refrained from asking Scissors any questions regarding his personal life or history. Sarah's direct question brought total silence to the table. "Grandpa," she asked, "Why do people call you Scissors? Don't you have a real name?"

Scissors smiled, "That's a good question, Sarah. Let me ask you one first. When you play with your dolls and Marley, do you pretend sometimes to be somebody else?"

Sarah nodded her agreement.

"Many years ago, I left my parents, my family and my country. When I arrived in the United States, I was alone and homeless. I didn't speak a word of English. The immigration officials couldn't pronounce my name so they gave me one in English. It didn't matter to me. I was beginning a new life with a new name. Most of my life, I used the name they gave me. During the last few years at Mencius House, because I am a barber, everyone there calls me Scissors. I like that very much. How we live each day of our lives has nothing to do with our names, so names have never been that important to me. But, I am very happy, Sarah, you gave me one more name. It's always wonderful to be called 'Grandpa.'"

"Time for dessert," Peggy announced. "Sarah and Tyler, will you please clear the table?"

Of course, there wasn't just one dessert. There was chocolate cake, rhubarb pie, ice cream and apple pie. After a second small piece of apple pie, Scissors declared it probably was the best he had ever eaten. After so much food, everyone agreed a short walk would be a good idea. When they returned, there was time for a few games. As the evening came to a close, Tyler, Peggy and Ron invited Scissors for Christmas. Sarah chimed in with a "Please come."

Scissors smiled broadly, "How can I refuse my granddaughter? Thank you all for everything."

Chapter VII

Tyler saw Scissors on Saturdays and gave him duplicate copies of all the pictures Maria had taken on Thanksgiving. Four weeks flew by and Tyler and Maria picked up Scissors on Christmas Eve. He carried a small black suitcase and a fairly large package.

After a nice dinner, the family and Scissors went to a Christmas midnight candlelight service at their church. It had snowed lightly during the day leaving a thin blanket of white to reflect the lights, which illuminated the main path. The stars were out. There was no wind. It truly was a night of peace. With closed eyes, Tyler expressed his thanks for all his blessings and prayed for the health and safety of all his loved ones, his family, Maria, Jason and his other friends, Scissors, and all those who lived and worked at Mencius House. He thought of the Collector, Bones, Bo, and the Bottleman. He prayed that the Cat Lady was safe, well and loved.

Christmas was fun from dawn to dusk. In the morning, the adults spent most of their time watching the youngsters open gifts. There were even a few gifts under the tree for Scissors. After all the gifts were opened, Scissors pointed out one more present. Sarah went and got it. The tag said, "To the Smith Family."

Sarah couldn't wait to see what was inside but she and Tyler took their time unwrapping the gift. It was a painting. A beautiful oil painting—a collage of children's faces. One of the faces was Sarah's. One by one the family held the painting enjoying the beauty and innocent wisdom of each child. Tyler slowly raised his eyes to look at the old man. Although he asked Scissors a question, he was really stating a fact. "You painted this magnificent picture, didn't you?"

"Yes, Tyler," Scissors replied. "I hope you and your family like it."

With the exception of Tyler, Scissors' answer was a complete surprise to everyone. Everyone told Scissors how much they loved the painting. They would treasure it. Sarah got up and gave her "Grandpa" a kiss on the cheek. The adults realized Scissors had exceptional talent and began asking him about how and when he had learned to paint.

Scissors related that his mother had been very artistic and he had painted for fun for many years. It made him very happy when friends enjoyed his efforts. A few minutes later, Maria arrived with her folks; they too were enthralled with Scissors' painting. Maria began snapping more pictures.

It was a wonderful Christmas for Scissors. It was a wonderful Christmas for everyone. When it was time for Scissors to go, everyone hugged and kissed him. He had become a member of two families. They all hoped to see him soon. Once again, they told him they would cherish his beautiful painting. Scissors knew they meant it.

Scissors was always at peace. He loved people, but as they left the house and he took Maria and Tyler's arms, he knew the past two days had been very special.

New Year's passed along with the first semester, George Washington's birthday and St. Patrick's day. Tyler was busy with schoolwork, T'ai Chi, Maria and Mencius House on Saturdays. After his regular responsibilities, he would meet with the Collector.

On the last Saturday in March, Tyler entered Mencius House. Many people greeted him including Scissors who would be returning home with Tyler at the end of the day. As he worked his way toward the kitchen, Bo Peterson came out of the conference room looking rather glum.

"Why the long face, Bo?" Tyler asked.

"Remember the property we hoped to someday purchase to build a larger and better shelter?" Bo asked. "We had first refusal, but a broker called me yesterday. He had an offer. It was much more than we could ever match so the property was sold. I know our search team won't give up but I don't have a lot of hope."

Tyler listened sympathetically and nodded his understanding of the magnitude of the loss. He gave Bo a pat on the back before continuing his trip to the kitchen to join in preparing breakfast. Later that day, Tyler met the Collector in the meeting room. They waited a short time to get online to check Mencius House's e-mail. It took only a few minutes to read and respond to the e-mail and make notes.

The Collector changed the subject, "Tyler, today is special. In half an hour, regional, state and national conferences regarding the plight of the homeless will begin. All the meetings will be linked together via satellite and the internet simultaneously. Every agenda will include discussions on needed legislation and effective programs to help the millions that have no place to call home."

Just before the hour, Rabbit, Bones, Donna, Bo Peterson and other volunteers came into the room. The Collector flicked on the TV channel that was to carry the opening ceremonies of the World Conference on the Homeless. After an opening prayer, the chairwoman of the conference introduced the first speaker, the United States Ambassador to the United Nations. A tall gray-haired man moved to the podium.

The Ambassador began his remarks. "Children, Ladies and Gentlemen of our planet. We are together this week to devise, develop, and find the means of implementing programs to improve the lives of millions of human beings—human beings that are tragically homeless. May your love and compassion bring hope and a future to those who believe they have no future.

"I am here today, too, as a father, a father who had lost a daughter he never expected to see again. She is here today with her children and grandchildren. They, too, believed their mother and Nana was gone forever. I have asked her to say a few words because I know her recent experience is especially relevant to the purpose that brings us all together."

A well-dressed, attractive, middle aged lady moved toward the microphone. A younger man and woman guided two children to stand on either side of the older lady. Each child held a contented cat. When the older lady reached the microphone, she looked directly into the eyes of everyone who was watching. Tyler, the Collector and Bones were stunned. They stared, speechless, at the television screen.

"My friends," she began, "My name is Marion. These are my children, Barbara and Frank and two of my grandchildren, Kelley and Doug. Several years ago, I lost my husband to cancer. It was a horrible and devastating blow for our family. For my son, Tim, it was a loss he could not accept, and Tim took his own life to be with Dad. My two losses were beyond my emotional strength to cope. I left my home and family—physically and mentally. Overnight, the world I had known was replaced by two other worlds—the world of the mentally ill and the world of the homeless.

"For over two years, I was barely aware of my existence. I survived in a subway station, thanks to the compassion and love of many other human beings. Hanna, a bag lady, found me, shared her pushcart and subway spot. She was an alcoholic, yet she reached out to me and kept me safe until others took over my care. Hanna passed away. A man I simply know as the Collector began looking after me. He and others brought me food as I huddled all day behind our pushcart wall with two stray cats. One day a young man repaired a flashlight for me that I had brought from home. When I was able to turn on the light, I reread the inscription from my children and at that moment, it seemed I was able to once again turn on my life and face my memories, which had driven me to the streets.

"For all street people, I thank everyone who works with and shows compassion for the homeless. They make it possible for miracles to happen. I'm a mother and grandmother again because there are some good samaritans in this world. I know becoming homeless could happen to anyone. God bless."

No one in the Shelter's conference room said a word. Tears ran down the cheeks of everyone. On the television screen another person was speaking, but at Mencius House no one was listening. Each person knew they would never forget the Cat Lady's resurrection and her words.

"You must be very happy, Collector," Tyler commented. "You not only saved the Cat Lady's life but changed the lives of all who love her."

"It wasn't only me, my friend," the Collector mused. "It certainly was wonderful to see that, at least once in a while, there are happy endings. The Cat Lady was lucky to find herself. I know she will cherish every new day in her life. Sadly, the majority of street people endure a lonely, difficult existence for too many years. You know, Tyler, it's funny. I didn't see any indication she was capable of changing. Maybe that flashlight was the spark or shock that brought her back to reality?"

Tyler shrugged his shoulders. "Just a coincidence, I'm sure," he said.

Tyler's answer had been quick, yet he was still thinking. He remembered fixing a floor lamp. He remembered the dream he had before waking up from the coma. In his mind, again he could clearly see Meng K'e standing before him and hearing his words about light and messengers. Once more, he asked himself—was that experience real or my imagination? Doubts still remained. The flashlight must have been just another coincidence.

"Collector, before we leave," Tyler asked, "do you happen to know who Mencius was? I've surfed the internet, searched in libraries but have never found anything about a person with that name." The Collector looked at Tyler quizzically. At first, he thought Tyler was joking. Tyler was serious. The Collector was puzzled.

"My computer is still humming," the Collector said. "Let's see if we can find anything in its encyclopedia."

Tyler shook his head. He told the Collector that he had the same encyclopedia in his computer. He turned away, packed his stuff in his backpack and prepared to leave for home. He turned his head and once more glanced at Collector's computer. Tyler froze. He was astonished as he read the text that appeared on the screen . . .

"MENCIUS (371? - 289 BC)"

"The philosopher Mencius was considered the second Chinese sage after Confucius. He believed in the essential goodness of human nature— the thinking heart.

His views on government and economics are so remarkable that they find wide acceptance in the 20th century. He stated his thesis as: The people are the most important element in a nation: the spirits of the land and grain come next: the sovereign counts the least.

The book MENCIUS is a collection of sayings and stories. He believed man could attain oneness with the universe by perfecting his own moral nature. He had absolute faith in the moral purpose of the universe. For more than one thousand years he has been regarded as the cofounder of Confucianism. Mencius is the latinized name of Meng K'e." [*]

Without speaking, Tyler sat down in a chair and read the screen again. Finally, he leaned back, closed his eyes and smiled. This information had been in his computer or could be found in any library. He simply had not been allowed to see it. "Yes, Meng K'e. I do believe," he mused. "No more doubts, I promise."

The Collector could pretty much guess Tyler's thoughts. "My young friend," he began "I believe knowledge is often hidden from us until we are able to accept and partially understand it. It certainly took a lot of hard knocks and wrong turns before I listened to my heart. Take care."

Scissors was reading at a table, waiting for Tyler.

"Sorry to keep you waiting, Grandpa," Tyler apologized. "Let's go home and have a wonderful weekend."

"No problem, Tyler," Scissors replied. "Time stops when I am reading. I'm trying to learn a little about Chinese philosophy. I believe this shelter was named after a Chinese philosopher."

Tyler grinned and, without thinking, said, "It figures! I mean, I think you are right, Grandpa— very right."

---

[*] MENCIUS Translated by D.C. Lau, Penguin Books, London England 1970

Scissors spent many delightful weekends and holidays with the Smiths and Cugnos during the Spring and joined them on extended trips in the summer. He became Grandpa to everyone.

Tyler and Maria found it difficult to believe that more than a year had passed. Their second summer together they pounded more nails for Habitat, dated, and took Scissors on family trips. They were now seniors and began their final year of high school. Maria and her team continued to tutor at Mencius House. Tyler's Fall Saturdays were spent on the soccer field. Maria often brought Scissors to the games. Scissors would stay overnight. He and Tyler would return to Mencius House on Sunday. The Collector kept Tyler up-to-date via e-mail. The Shelter was now turning away over one hundred people each day. There was no news regarding funds for another facility. Tyler could see that Bo Peterson was worried and working too hard.

Maria waited outside the boys' locker room for Tyler. It had been the last game of the soccer season. Thanksgiving was tomorrow. Maria had driven to Mencius House before the game to pick up Scissors for the holiday. Finally, Tyler emerged chatting with a couple of friends. He saw Maria and hurried to her.

Maria spoke with a worried voice, "When I arrived at Mencius House, Rabbit was waiting for me. He handed me letters Scissors had left for us. Rabbit seemed upset and simply told me Scissors wanted us to open the letters together. He told me Scissors had come by earlier in the week and gave everyone a hug and a kiss good-bye. All he said was 'We'll meet again.' As always, he wouldn't say more. What do you think, Tyler?"

"I don't want to guess: Let's go sit down and read the letters," Tyler suggested.

Sitting side by side the young couple read their letters in silence. The letters were almost the same. Scissors wrote that he loved them and their families very much. All the holidays and weekends he had been with them had been wonderful, very special and some of the happiest days of his life. He was very proud of Maria and Tyler for their school achievements but also for their compassion and willingness to give of themselves to help others. He hoped they would make this philosophy a cornerstone in their lives. He closed the letter with—

"Until we meet again—with love,

Grandpa Scissors."

There was a postscript. "I hope you both will accept my invitation."

Maria was upset. In a quivering voice she asked, "Tyler, what do you think?"

"I believe," Tyler hesitantly began, "We will not see Scissors again—in this world. Scissors must be very ill."

Maria began to cry. Tyler held her as tears also trickled down his cheeks.

Chapter IX

It was a sad Thanksgiving at the Smith and Cugno houses. Tyler was in constant touch with the Collector. No one at the Shelter had seen or heard from Scissors. Early in December, after finishing supper and the dishes had been put away, Tyler went right to his room to begin work on a newly assigned physics project. The day's mail lay beside his computer. A small envelope was on top of the pile. Inside was a engraved formal invitation.

Just as Tyler finished reading, the phone rang. It was Maria. She had been crying. She, too, held an invitation in her hands. The next morning Tyler called Bo Peterson but before he could ask a question, Bo began talking.

"Tyler, you won't believe what I am about to tell you. Last week an attorney from a big law firm came by and informed me of a bequest by a gentleman who had recently passed away. The gentleman had set aside a sum of money to buy new clothes for each child and adult who lives or eats at Mencius House. The lawyer said new clothes meant shoes, boots, underwear, shirts, and pants, winter coats, hats, gloves, etc. I said that it would cost thousands. The attorney said he realized that and an account in Mencius House's name had been opened at the largest department store in the city. My staff and volunteers are to buy the clothes as soon as possible. That's not all. Our benefactor wants to give a Christmas party for everyone at Mencius House including volunteers and twenty invited guests. The lawyer said his firm will arrange everything, including supplying the food, a staff to serve it and presents for the children. For some of our kids and maybe a few of the adults, this may be their first happy Christmas. Can you believe it, Tyler?"

You are cordially invited to the graduation supper of D.P.B. and Christmas Party December 18th at 5:00 p.m. at Mencius House

Tyler spoke into the phone and tried to sound surprised, "That's amazing, Bo—it's wonderful. By the way, what is the date of the Christmas Party?"

"Just a minute, Tyler," Bo answered. "I've got it in my notes somewhere. Right, here it is. December 18th at 5:00 p.m. I hope you can make it. I'm only sorry Scissors won't be here to join the party."

"Thanks, Bo," Tyler said. "Maria and I will be there and as for Scissors—I have a feeling he will be there, too. Take care, Bo. We'll see you soon."

Bo Peterson slowly put down the phone. He wondered why Tyler hadn't heard Scissors had passed on.

Chapter X

Often on Sunday afternoons Maria and Tyler studied together, but today was December 18th. As they drove to Mencius House, both wondered what the evening had in store. Tyler thought there might be a surprise or two. There were to be more surprises than he could have imagined.

Their first surprise was when they walked through the Shelter's front door. A chubby Santa Claus greeted them with a "Merrrrry Christmas" and deep, "Ho, Ho, Ho," which sounded a lot like Bones. The dining room was decorated from floor to ceiling as a winter fantasyland. A formally dressed trio played seasonal music on a violin, harp and flute. Children and adults were looking for their names on place cards at the tables. Everyone's eyes kept returning to the large beautifully trimmed Christmas tree, which sparkled and twinkled in the far corner. Beneath its branches, there were lots of presents—this fact was not lost on the children.

The Collector rolled up, looking like one of Santa's helpers. His smile was even bigger than usual. "Welcome to a Christmas Miracle. Our mysterious benefactor has supplied everything you see from soup to nuts. Tyler, you and the other volunteers won't have to lift a finger tonight. Your names are on place cards. Have fun—I'll join you shortly."

Maria gave the Collector a kiss. Tyler grinned and told the Collector he should be that lucky. Laughing, Maria and Tyler began to look for their places. They noticed every child and adult wore new clothes from their shoes or sneakers to their elf caps. As they hunted for their places, they saw many familiar faces: Residents, volunteers, Tyrone from the bank, Rabbit and Bo Peterson. The well-known face of the state's female senior senator was a surprise. She was standing behind her chair talking with a man who appeared to be a rabbi. A few minutes later Maria found her place. The lady seated next to her introduced herself. Her name was Alicia and she was a minister, as well as being Tyrone's better half. She winked after her comment.

Tyler found his chair. The Collector would be on his left and a gentleman with a neat black beard wearing a flowing white robe stood on his right. He smiled and offered his hand to Tyler. He spoke with an Indian accent.

"I am Swami Yogananda. Tyler, I have heard quite a bit about you."

Tyler returned the Swami's greeting and asked how the Swami knew of him. The Swami's answer was incomplete. "We have a mutual friend." At that moment, Bo Peterson picked up the microphone beside the Christmas tree.

"My friends" he began, "I still do not know whom we can thank for this wonderful evening and the gifts, which Santa will distribute. Hopefully, we will learn later. Before the food is served, I would like to ask our guests who represent different religions to say a few words."

Spiritual leaders of the city rose. . . two women and four men: a Catholic, a Hindu, a Jew, a Protestant, a Muslim and a Buddhist came together in front of the balsam pine. One by one, through brief stories, they shared their belief in the Creator's love for each and every person. When they had finished, the kitchen door opened. Whole roast turkeys and bowls of mashed potatoes, vegetables, stuffing, and gravy were carried into the room by a small army of smiling strangers.

Conversation at the tables almost ceased as people enjoyed the delicious food. During the meal, Tyler had a chance to talk with Swami Yogananda. He asked how the Swami happened to be present. The Swami said he had known the evening's sponsor for many years. Smiling, he added the gentleman hadn't been a Hindu but certainly qualified as an honorary Yogi. In response to Tyler's question, the Swami described a Yogi.

"Our bible, the Bavagad Gita says," the Swami quoted, " 'He is truly a yogi, who, on this earth and up to the time of his death, is able to master every impulse of desire and wrath. He is a happy man.' I believe that describes our friend."

Tyler swallowed hard. There was no longer any doubt in his mind. He knew the name of their mutual friend.

After dessert, a well-dressed woman carrying a rectangular package approached the microphone. Slowly, with the help of a youngster, she removed the wrapping paper from a large acrylic painting. It was a superb painting—a collage of faces, children and adults.

The woman spoke in a strong but gentle voice, "Before Santa distributes the presents under the tree, I would like to give all of you this gift from the man who is responsible for this evening. I am sure when you look closely at the painting you will recognize many people. They are the faces of Mencius House. One of those faces is the face of the artist—my grandfather—Dante Pietro Bellini—you called him Scissors."

For a few moments there was complete silence. Some adults cried. Finally, everyone rose and applauded. A stunned Bo Peterson walked over to the woman. He shook her hand and accepted the painting. He barely was able to ask Santa to take over while he, invited guests, and Scissors' granddaughter met in the conference room.

Maria and Tyler joined the people moving toward the conference room. No one spoke. All wondered what was about to unfold. Everyone sat down except the woman.

"Ladies and Gentlemen," the woman began. "My name is Joan Bellini Whalen. I am an attorney and the executor of my grandfather's trust—the Dante P. Bellini Foundation.

"Grandpa dictated the invitation you received. The words were chosen carefully. He said exactly what he believed. My grandfather was convinced that our soul does not die but rather graduates after our earthly experience to another dimension to continue our spiritual journey. Grandpa was certain that we shall all meet again.

"When my grandfather arrived in this country he spoke no English. The immigration official who did not understand Italian wrote his name down as Dan Bell. A few weeks later, Dan Bell was a hod carrier toting bricks twelve hours a day, six days a week. When he had free time, he cut people's hair—a trade he learned in Italy. He never would accept money for giving a haircut, although I understand he gratefully accepted meals and apple pies. One day a beautiful young woman, who was the daughter of one his 'free' haircut customers, gave him a pie. Her name was Sarah."

Everyone smiled.

Joan continued, "Dan Bell worked hard, taught himself English and learned the construction business fast, and he earned a reputation as an honest, dependable, highly skilled and conscientious worker. He married Sarah. In less than five years, he had his own construction company, which grew at a staggering rate. His fine wife handled all the bookkeeping and financial transactions. He worked harder than his best man. He knew how to treat people. His employees would do anything for him, and their attitude made it possible for Grandpa to make a lot of money. In a few short years, Grandpa and Grandma were very wealthy. Dante had learned the formula for being successful. He also learned that he didn't know much about anything else so he began to devote every free moment to educating himself. He became an avid reader. Grandpa's four loves during his life were his wife Sarah, reading, growing roses, and painting.

"Grandpa married in his mid-twenties. Sarah and Dan had three children during their happy forty-two year marriage. When Grandpa was in his fifties, he had his name legally changed back to Bellini.

"Throughout his life he invested his money wisely, starting many successful businesses and eventually funding young entrepreneurs. By the age of sixty, he was a multi-millionaire and began to study how best his money could be used to help other people. A number of you are here tonight because Dante supports the work you are doing.

"Grandpa never wrote out checks, no matter how respected the cause or institution, without doing considerable research. First, he would visit the institution and talk with its custodians, nurses, doctors, patients, clients, and administrators and actually participate in programs. Only after a great deal of thought would he donate money. He wanted it to be wisely spent, helping people in need.

"I have brought you up to this moment. During the past several years, Grandpa spent a lot of time here at Mencius House. He came to love and respect the residents, staff and volunteers. He wants your good work to continue and expand. He set up a Mencius House Trust. There are sufficient monies in the trust to allow you to renovate this building, improve services here and build a brand new, even larger shelter for long-term assistance and rehabilitation programs. This facility can be built on a parcel of property nearby that Grandpa bought months ago.

"Grandpa instructed me to ask many of you to serve on the first Board of Directors of the new shelter and that Bo Peterson remain as the director of both shelters. Of course, Mr. Peterson, there are funds for the additional staff you will need and a much-deserved raise for yourself. In addition, Grandpa wanted the board to always have at least two high school students as full members. Of course, Maria and Tyler, your Grandpa named you. He assured me you would accept.

"Again, let me say, the trust has more than sufficient funds to allow you to do all I have described and maintain the two shelters for as long as they are needed. Grandpa wants them to remain places of compassion and hope. Ladies and Gentlemen—Scissors sends his love."

No one moved. Joan Bellini Whalen began introducing herself to each person and passing out legal documents. Bo Peterson, Bones, the Collector and the guests who had known Dante Pietro Bellini willingly accepted Scissors' request to serve on the Board of Directors. Tyler and Maria's hearts were full of love for the man who, in a short time, had become so important in their lives. Somehow they felt Scissors would continue to watch over them. Wouldn't their parents be surprised to hear the life story of their families' adopted Grandpa.

Chapter XI

In college, Tyler's major was world medicine. He studied products, treatments, and herbs used to treat diseases and ailments from all over the world. Maria and Tyler were married in their senior year and remained inseparable. Tyler earned a second degree in China, where he studied herbal medicine and acupuncture. He met with tribal medicine men in the jungles of Maylaysia and Brazil and with brilliant researchers from Europe and Australia. He became an authority on the latest discoveries, technologies and natural treatments that proved effective in healing old and new diseases. His web site was used by every medical facility on the planet from the newest city hospitals to one-doctor clinics in remote areas. Tyler believed science could help with the world's problems but only people with a "thinking heart" could solve them.

Maria and Tyler spent their honeymoon in the Philippines searching for Tyler's brother and sisters. The newly-weds were able to find one sister, Lucia, and a brother, Miguel. Tyler learned his mother had lost her husband in a volcano eruption and that an illness left her unable to care for her children so she was forced to place them in an orphanage. At the reunion, it seemed they had all known each other forever. Maria and Tyler and Tyler's Filipino family remained close throughout their lives. Usually, they visited every two or three years. Several of Tyler's nieces and nephews from the Philippines came to live and study with Tyler, Maria and their three children. The years went by, and eventually, Maria and Tyler had five grandchildren. All during their lives, Maria and Tyler maintained a close relationship with Mencius House.

Chapter XII

As Tyler's 78th birthday approached, his active day grew longer by choice. He slept less and added another artistic passion to his life—sculpting faces of children. Maria, his wonderful wife for fifty years, had passed on. Their three children were married and lived within a few hours' drive, so he could see their grandchildren often.

One autumn morning, while he was working on a new sculpture, a middle-aged couple came to his front door. They introduced themselves as the Horners.

"Dr. Smith," David Horner began, "we are sorry to bother you, and maybe this is a wild goose chase, but do you repair lamps as a hobby?"

"First, please come in," Tyler requested. "Yes, I try to fix lamps but haven't repaired one in years."

"Well," Mrs. Horner continued, "this is going to sound weird, but we have this old lamp of my mother's. It has been in our family for generations. I don't remember it ever working, but Mom has asked us to please get it fixed. She is very old, and imagines seeing and speaking with ancestors and loved ones who have passed on. She said your name was given to her and only you could fix this lamp. We have no idea how she heard of you. To be honest, we tried several appliance repair shops near our home but they all said this lamp could not be fixed. The lamp is not important to me, but my mother is very important. She has done so much for so many. We couldn't give up on this lamp without at least finding you. We searched through a number of telephone directories before discovering your address. When awake, Mom is lucid and sharp as ever. She always asks if we have had the lamp fixed. When we say no, she becomes quite agitated. We will be happy to pay you for your time to look at it."

Tyler smiled. It had been a long time. "Of course, I will be happy to see what I can do," Tyler offered. "I will do my best, but I cannot accept any money."

It was a pretty little lamp with a Tiffany-like glass shade—it might even have been a Tiffany. No matter, Tyler knew it was a special lamp. The wiring and most of the metal parts were corroded, but it certainly appeared repairable. Taking his time, the old man spent hours cleaning, replacing parts and installing a new cord and plug in the antique lamp. Finally, when he pushed the switch, there was light—a warm, bright light.

Late in the afternoon, Tyler made a telephone call. He put on a heavy coat before leaving to drive to the Horners.

The Horners greeted Tyler warmly. They thanked him sincerely for repairing the old lamp.

"I know Mom will be very happy to have the lamp beside her." Mrs. Horner commented. "It will definitely make a difference." She excused herself for a moment and then reappeared with a freshly baked apple strudel. Tyler smiled and thanked Mrs. Horner—the strudel looked delicious. They all shook hands and said their good-byes.

Slowly, the old man walked back to his car and paused before opening the door. Above him a street light cast a soft, golden glow on everything below. Tyler raised his head. Looking at the light, he thought of all those who had touched his life, especially his loved ones: Maria, their children, his parents, the Collector, Jason, Grandpa Scissors, Meng K'e and many others—lives that would be intertwined with his forever. Tyler knew they were all near and the words of one of his favorite writers, Richard Bach, author of *Jonathan Livingston Seagull*, came to mind.

> *"When we come to the last moment of this lifetime, and we look back across it, the only thing that's going to matter is 'what was the quality of our love?'"*

Tyler's silent contemplation was replaced by a vision of the child's face he was creating in clay. He smiled and spoke out loud to no one he could see but to all those he knew were listening, "Well, my friends, time to go home; I still have work to do."

THE END.